First published in the United States, Great Britain, Canada, Australia, and New Zealand in 2011
by North-South Books Inc., an imprint of NordSüd Verlag AG, CH-8005 Zürich, Switzerland.
Distributed in the United States by North-South Books Inc., New York 10001.

Library of Congress Cataloging-in-Publication Data is available.
Printed in Germany by Grafisches Centrum Cuno GmbH & Co. KG, 39240 Calbe, April 2011.
ISBN: 978-0-7358-4033-1 (trade edition)
1  3  5  7  9  •  10  8  6  4  2

www.northsouth.com

FSC
®
.fsc.org

Rick de Haas

# Peter
## and the
# Winter Sleepers

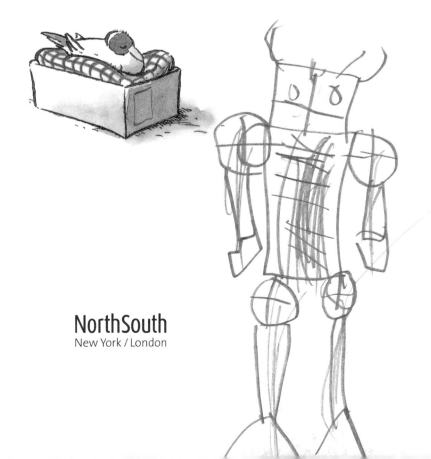

NorthSouth
New York / London

Peter lived in a lighthouse with his grandmother and his dog, Leo. One morning Peter woke up earlier than usual. His room was lit by a strange light. Curious, Peter pulled the curtain aside.

It had been snowing! Not the dirty, wet snow like they usually got. This snow was the real thing!

Peter dressed in a flash and ran out of the lighthouse.

"Come on, Leo!" he called. "We're going to make snowmen!"

They played outside the whole day. That evening it began to snow again.

"From the look of the sky, there will be a lot more snow," said Grandma. "I'd better bring the chicken and the goat inside."

Grandma was right. The next morning the snow was three feet deep.

"Hmmm," said Peter. "I hear scratching at the front door, but I can't see anybody."

Peter opened the door. Outside was a
high wall of snow. In that wall was a hole.
And in that hole sat a very cold rabbit.
"Quick! Come in!" said Peter.

"I guess you've never had a winter like this one," said
Peter. "Well, neither have I. You can sleep here till it's
over. Here's a little bed for you."

As he was making the rabbit cozy, Peter heard
another sound. Something was tapping at the window.

It was an owl, just as cold as the rabbit had been.

"Come join us," said Peter. "There's plenty of room."

"And plenty of food too," said Grandma.

Day after day, more sleepers arrived.

Some on their own.

Some in pairs.

And others with their whole family!
Peter made each of them a small bed on the
stairs. Everyone wanted to sleep in the lighthouse
till the snow was gone.

Well, almost everyone. Some of the
animals were wide-awake at night. They kept
Peter awake too.

And the snow kept right on falling. It was
no longer possible to play outside. Peter
was beginning to think that enough was enough.

It was Peter's job to clean the hall. The stairs were nearly full now. Thank goodness there had been no new guests for the past few days. Then Peter heard a noise at the front door.

"A fox!" said Peter. "How nice. We don't have a fox yet. Do come in. It must be lonely for you out there with all your friends here in the lighthouse."

The fox sat down on the floor.

"Stay," said Elmo. "I'm going to find you a bed.

You wait here downstairs."

Elmo walked up the stairs.

"Another animal has arrived," he told Grandma.

Grandma sighed. "We already have a full house," she said. "There are droppings everywhere. And it smells. I had to open a window up here. We're running out of food too. What does the newcomer eat, do you think?"

"I'm not sure," said Peter. "It's a fox."

"A fox!" said Grandma. "Is that a good idea? Foxes eat rabbits. And mice and birds . . ."

Suddenly Peter heard a rustle behind him.
"I told you to wait downstairs!" he yelled. "What are you doing in Gull's bed? Where is Gull?

"What have you done?!

"My gull is not for eating!
Out! Get out of here now!"

Peter chased the fox out of the lighthouse. Then he looked up. What a surprise. The sun was shining, and the sky was bright blue. And there was Gull!

"Oh, Gull," said Peter. "You were outside all the time. Did you see the sun shining again?"

Then Peter had an awful thought. The fox. Where had he gone?

Grandma pointed to the snowbank.
"Look! He has fallen into a hole. He can't
get out by himself. We must save him!"

So Peter crawled out on the ladder, and Grandma crawled out behind him and held his feet. Together, they were just long enough to reach the fox.

"Come back, Fox," said Peter. "It was all a mistake. You can stay as long as you like. And you can pick out your own bed. I promise."

Gull had been right. The weather was changing. The snow was starting to melt and spring was in the air.

One by one, the guests left, until all the winter sleepers were gone.

All except for one.

"I'm sorry, Leo," said Peter. "But I promised him.
And you have to keep your promises, don't you?"